SESAME STREET

D0211853

A Perfect Picnic

By Sarah Albee
Illustrated by Tom Brannon

"Sesame Workshop"®, "Sesame Street"®, and associated characters, trademarks, and design elements are owned and licensed by Sesame Workshop. ©2006, 2010 Sesame Workshop. All Rights Reserved.

The DALMATIAN PRESS and PIGGY TOES PRESS names and logos are trademarks of Dalmatian Publishing Group, Atlanta, Georgia 30329. No part of this book may be reproduced or copied in any form without written permission from the copyright owner. All rights reserved.

Printed in Dongguan, Guangdong, China

10 11 12 13 SF 36041 10 9 8 7 6 5 4 3 2 1
Sesame Street Handle Box Set Book: A Perfect Picnic

"It's a perfect day for a picnic!" said Bert.
"What a fine way to celebrate spring.
Smell those spring flowers! See the lambs in the field!
Feel that breeze! Hear those cute birdies sing!"

“Look!” Ernie said. “There’s a baseball game!”
Elmo smiled. “And a bicycle race!”
“Ah, springtime,” said Bert as he set down the basket.
“This looks like a nice, quiet place.”

Zoe brought over some flowers.
It was then that Bert started to sneeze.
"*Achoo!*" said Bert. "All these spring blossoms . . .
ACHOO . . . give me . . . *COUGH* . . . allergies."

The gentle spring breeze began to pick up.
It blew away Zoe's bouquet,
And then all the napkins, the spoons, Ernie's hat . . .
Why, that wind nearly blew Bert away!

Just then the food started marching.
Off went the bread and the jam.
“The ANTS,” Bert cried, “are taking the food!
They just marched away with the ham!”

"Throw crumbs for the robins!" Elmo suggested.
So Bert began tossing out bread.
When they saw what was coming, the ants ran away.
But now there were birdies instead.

"This is *not* how I'd planned things!" Bert said with a sigh,
As chipmunks made off with his carrot.

A lamb ate some lettuce straight from Elmo's sandwich!
But Elmo was happy to share it.

CRACK! went a bat as it hit a baseball.
They all looked up at the sky.
That baseball came whizzing and hit with a *SPLAT!*
Right smack in the chocolate cream pie.

"Here come the racers!" Zoe announced.
"Look out, Bert! They're headed toward *you*!"
ZOOM! All the bicycles sped through a puddle,
Splashing Bert top to bottom with goo.

"Well, at least there's no rain on our spring celebration,"
Said Bert with another small sigh.
"Uh-oh." Ernie pointed as gray clouds rushed in.
Then raindrops poured down from the sky.

“Our spring picnic is ruined!” the others said sadly.
“The rainstorm has spoiled *everything*!”
Bert smiled just a little. “Now cheer up,” he said.
“Without rain . . .”

". . . it just wouldn't be spring!"

SESAME STREET

A Perfect Picnic

Ages 2 and up

Sesame Workshop, the nonprofit educational organization behind Sesame Street, puts the proceeds it receives from sales of its products right back into Sesame Street and its other projects for children at home and around the world.

Learn more at www.sesameworkshop.org

Piggy Toes Press

3101 Clairmont Rd., Ste. G
Atlanta, GA 30329
Printed in Dongguan, Guangdong, China

SF36041-0910